The
Cardinal's
Snuffbox

The Cardinal's Snuffbox

by Kenneth Roseman

illustrated by Bill Negron

Union of American Hebrew Congregations
New York

ISBN 0-8074-0059-9

Manufactured in the United States of America

4 5 6 7 8 9 0

The Cardinal's Snuffbox

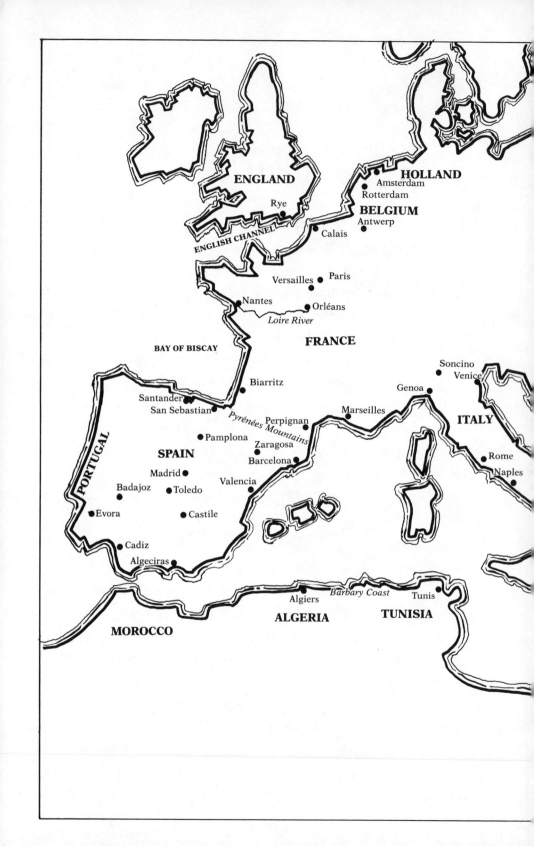

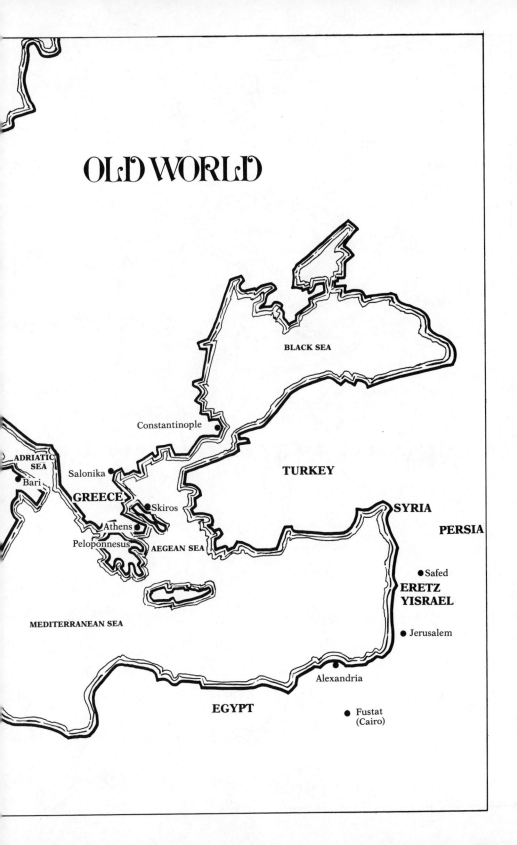

OLD WORLD

BLACK SEA

Constantinople

ADRIATIC
SEA

Salonika

Bari

TURKEY

SYRIA

PERSIA

GREECE

Skiros

Athens

Peloponnesus

AEGEAN SEA

Safed

ERETZ
YISRAEL

Jerusalem

MEDITERRANEAN SEA

Alexandria

EGYPT

Fustat
(Cairo)

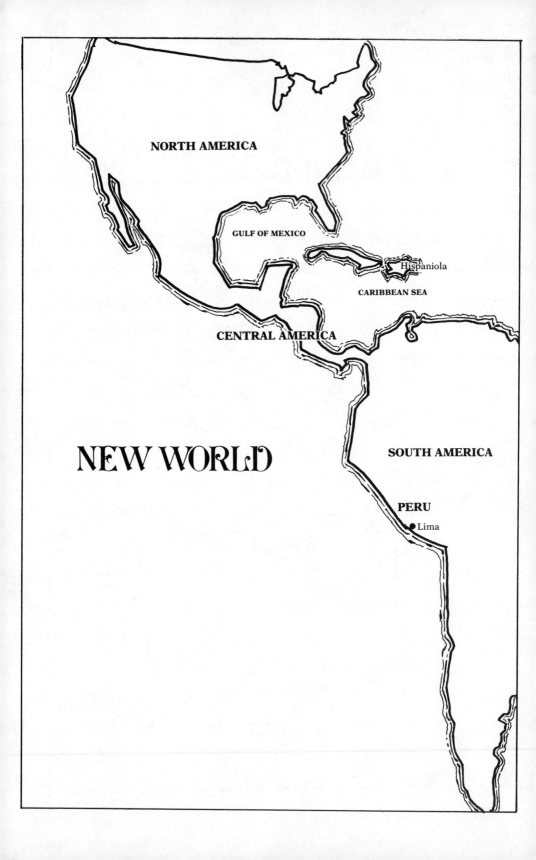

1

You are about to read a very different kind of book. With most books you start on page 1, and then turn to page 2, page 3, and so on, all in the proper order.

As you read this book, you'll do something different. Read the first four pages. At the bottom of page 4, you will find a choice. If you choose one way, the instructions tell you to turn to page 5; if you take the other road, you will be directed to page 6. Almost every page thereafter asks you to make the same kind of choice.

After you've read to the end of one series of choices, you can go back to an earlier part of the book and find out what would have happened if you had chosen differently.

There are many different stories in this book.

2

This book is historical fiction. The events you'll read about here are based on facts; the problems you'll face when you make your choices were once faced by real people. You may want to look in an atlas or refer to the maps included in this book while you read. That way, you can follow your journey as you make your choices through the book.

The careful reader will notice that several of the historical figures presented in this book lived more than a hundred years apart. On purpose, I have squeezed two centuries of Jewish history into a single lifetime to introduce you to a wide range of important Jewish people whose lives were greatly affected by the *Inquisition*.

As you come across words in italics, look them up in the glossary at the back of this book.

Now turn to page 3.

3

You are eleven years old and Jewish. You live in Madrid, a very important city in Spain. The year is 1492. Your father is an advisor to the King. The house you live in has a garden and patio circled with a high wall. Servants bring you anything you need. Your life has always been pleasant and comfortable.

Unfortunately for you, the *Inquisition* wants Spain to be a totally Catholic country. The *Inquisition* has been part of the Spanish Catholic Church since 1480. Its task is to make sure that members of the Church behave and believe correctly. When members of the *Inquisition* find someone who has not followed the right way, they can put that person in prison or force him or her to make a public confession. Every aspect of Spanish life is subject to careful scrutiny by the *Inquisition*; no one is safe from investigation. Nearly all Spaniards, Christians and Jews alike, are afraid of the *Inquisition*.

You do not know it yet, but the *Inquisition* has convinced *King Ferdinand* and *Queen Isabella* that Jews should no longer live in their kingdom. That way, the *Inquisition* will be able to exercise even more power and assure that Spain will be fully Catholic.

4

One night, your father comes home late. He seems very disturbed. He talks in a whisper with your mother. Then they call you and your sister and brother into the library. "Children," father says, "the King and Queen have passed a law that only Catholics may now live in Spain. They have told us that we must make a choice before the *Ninth of Av.* If we want to stay in Spain, we have to convert to Catholicism. If we want to remain Jewish, we must leave the country."

Your parents tell you that this decision is very important to your future. Your entire life will be affected by what you choose. They tell you to make your own choice, not necessarily to do what the rest of the family decides to choose.

You think very carefully. Then you make your decision.

☞ *If you choose to convert,
turn to page 5.*

☞ *If you choose to remain Jewish,
turn to page 6.*

5

You decide that you want to live in Spain, so you go to the Madrid Cathedral to convert. The priest questions you for an hour. After you convince him that you truly want to become a Catholic, he tells you that you have to study before you can be accepted as a convert. "After all," he tells you, "you have been a Jew for many years. Now you must learn to do things a different way."

He gives you a choice: go to live and study at a special school or study privately with him at the cathedral.

☞   *If you choose to go to the special school, turn to page 7.*

☞   *If you choose to study at the cathedral, turn to page 8.*

6

You decide to join the majority of Spanish Jews who have chosen to remain Jewish. "There have been tyrants before who have tried to make us give up our religion," says *Isaac Abravanel.* "These people are no different, but we won't give in. Let's move to another place where we are welcome as Jews."

Some of your parents' friends are convinced that they will be safest in Holland. Others are equally convinced that an eastward route through Italy, Greece, and Turkey is the right way to go.

☞ *If you go north toward Holland,*
turn to page 9.

☞ *If your choice is the eastward route,*
turn to page 10.

7

When you arrive at the boarding school, you discover other Jewish children who have also come to learn about Catholicism. The teachers are priests and are very strict. You begin to wonder whether you are doing the right thing. Sometimes, you think you should keep studying; at other times, you aren't sure and wonder if you should discuss your doubts with the other Jewish students.

☞   *If you keep studying,*
    turn to page 11.

☞   *If you discuss your doubts with other Jewish students,*
    turn to page 12.

8

When you arrive at the cathedral for the first lesson, you feel scared. Everything is foreign to you; it is very different from the synagogue.

The priest greets you warmly and takes you for a walk in the garden. He tells you not to be frightened. "Much of what we shall study is the same as in Judaism," he begins. "But there are some places where Judaism went wrong, and I'll try to show you where. You see, Judaism should have ended at the time of Jesus. He fulfilled the promises of the Jewish prophets. As a result, Judaism is no longer necessary."

You think about what the priest says. It sounds logical; perhaps he's right. You think again. Can it be that all the Jews of the last 1,500 years have been totally mistaken?

☞ *If you agree with the priest,
   turn to page 13.*

☞ *If you disagree and decide not to return for the next lesson,
   turn to page 14.*

9

You carry only those things that are most valuable to you —some money and jewels, clothing, and a few of your father's most precious Jewish books. You remember what your father often said: "As long as we have the *Torah* and the courage to plan and take risks, we can make a new life somewhere else."

When you reach the city of Santander, you pause. *Cardinal de Sourdes*, a leader of the Catholic Church, was once a friend of your father. Perhaps he would be willing to help. On the other hand, the Church is behind the *Inquisition*, and it agreed to the expulsion of the Jews. Will *Cardinal de Sourdes* help you or hurt you?

☞   *If you seek the Cardinal's assistance, turn to page 15.*

☞   *If you want to take your chances alone, turn to page 16.*

10

You carry only those things that are most valuable to you —some money and jewels, clothing, and a few of your father's most precious Jewish books.

You stow away on a Spanish ship headed for Constantinople. Each day is a dangerous challenge, sneaking out of your hiding place to find a few scraps of garbage to eat. If you are discovered, you'll be tossed overboard.

Along the way, your ship docks at the city of Venice. To leave the ship here might mean you'll go to prison! Yet Constantinople is a long way off. Prison in Venice might be far safer than the risks of traveling farther to the east. They wouldn't hold you for too long, and, after you get out of jail, life would not be bad at all.

Yet Constantinople is a large city, busy, wealthy, full of interesting sights. To live there would certainly be exciting. If you did get there, it probably would not be hard to leap ashore and make a new life for yourself.

From Constantinople, as well, *Eretz Yisrael* lies ahead. For nearly 1,500 years, Jews have prayed to return to *Zion*. The attraction is strong. Perhaps you should fulfill that urge to return.

☞   *If you abandon ship in Venice,*
     turn to page 26.

☞   *If you continue on toward Constantinople,*
     turn to page 17.

☞   *If Eretz Yisrael is your ultimate destination,*
     turn to page 18.

11

You find your classes difficult, but you've made up your mind to succeed. Pretty soon, you're at the head of your class. Because you are such a good student, the head of the school calls you into his office.

"My child," he says, "I don't want you to be afraid. You've done so well in your classes that I'm able to offer you a wonderful choice. We in the Church think you should join the Catholic clergy. One of our religious orders might be just right for you.

"On the other hand, you may not feel that God especially wants you to have a religious career in the Church. You might prefer a position as an officer in the King's army."

☞ *If you choose to enter a religious order,* *turn to page 19.*

☞ *If you select officer training,* *turn to page 20.*

12

You and your friends arrange to meet in a cellar late at night. It is dangerous to talk about Judaism now that Jews have been expelled from Spain by royal order. But you have come to trust each other, and you need to talk about your private feelings.

Some in the group are certain that you are doing the right thing. "There is no future for Jews in Spain, maybe in all of Europe. It is good to convert to Catholicism."

Others are not so sure. "Jews have been persecuted before, but we always remained loyal to God. We shouldn't abandon our faith now."

☞ *If you think it is right to convert,*
   turn to page 21.

☞ *If you think it is a mistake,*
   turn to page 22.

13

Sunday morning you go to church. It's your first experience of a mass, but the priest has prepared you well. You know what to expect and how to behave.

After services, you don't leave the church. You walk around and explore the building. In a small side room, you find piles of books, all in Hebrew. They have been taken from Jewish schools. To read them is illegal. You open one anyway. It's a prayer book. You begin to read. Then you hear footsteps.

The priest enters the room and is startled to see you. "What are you doing in here?" You feel trapped.

You turn toward the priest. "Father, forgive me. I was wandering through the building and found this room. My curiosity got the best of me, so I went in and started to look through these books. I didn't know I was doing anything wrong."

☞   *If you think the priest believes your apology,
     turn to page 23.*

☞   *If you don't believe you have convinced him,
     turn to page 24.*

14

But if you don't go back to the cathedral, where can you go? The priest will report you. And, if he doesn't, someone else will. Everyone is suspected of being an informer for the *Inquisition*. For a while, you live in back alleys and you steal garbage. But this can't last.

Somehow, you've got to leave Madrid. There are two routes—both risky. One is toward the sea; the other leads to the hills. Which will you take?

☞   *If you head toward the sea,
    turn to page 25.*

☞   *If you choose the hills,
    turn to page 54.*

15

The Cardinal receives you with friendship. "Child of my good friend, what may I do for you?" he asks.

You explain that you are afraid to travel without protection. Many dishonest people will try to take advantage of refugees. "Your Eminence," you say, "can you give me a letter of protection so that people will not harm me?"

"I can offer you two choices," the Cardinal replies. "If you wait here, a ship of mine will be leaving in a few weeks. It will carry you across the Bay of Biscay. But you're on your own until then. I cannot protect you openly. If I do, the *Inquisition* might suspect me—even me!—of not being a faithful Catholic.

"Or, I shall give you a letter of protection, sealed with my ring, and my own *snuffbox*. These should make it possible for you to cross the mountains safely."

☞ *If you wait for the ship,*
turn to page 27.

☞ *If you decide to move on immediately,*
turn to page 28.

16

The Cardinal may have been a friend of your father's, but that was long ago. *De Sourdes* is still a cardinal, a prince of the Catholic Church, and maybe even part of the *Inquisition*. Better to take your chances alone.

You think of ways to leave Santander. Since you've decided not to ask the Cardinal for a letter of protection, the land route over the Pyrénées seems too dangerous. One possibility is to go across the Bay of Biscay to the French city of Nantes; a ship is almost ready to sail in that direction. Or, you can wait, hoping that another vessel will carry you to an even safer destination.

☞   *If you decide on the ship for Nantes,*
    turn to page 29.

☞   *If you prefer to take the risks of waiting,*
    turn to page 30.

17

The harbor of Constantinople is crowded, noisy, and confusing. You decide to find a synagogue where you can thank God for bringing you safely to Turkey. Perhaps at the synagogue you can meet people who will help you get settled. You wander the bazaar-lined streets. Soon you are in the Jewish quarter. But there are so many synagogues, you don't know which to choose.

Suddenly, a synagogue name strikes you—B'nai Sepharad, "Sons of Spain." That's the one! And it is. . . . Most members are people like yourself who had to flee from Spain.

A member of the congregation, *Solomon Ashkenazi*, befriends you. "Young man," he says, "come home with me. I'll introduce you to two friends of mine who can help you. One is a merchant, the other a fine tailor and clothier."

☞   *If you decide to become a merchant,*
     turn to page 31.

☞   *If clothing is your choice,*
     turn to page 32.

18

The ship docks in Constantinople and, in your hope to find a way to *Eretz Yisrael*, you seek out other Jews.

At services the next day, you are repeatedly struck by the words of the *Amidah*, "ve'al Yerushalayim," "and upon Jerusalem." Right then and there, you know that you've made the right choice. You must fulfill the hope expressed by Jews every day since the *destruction of the Temple* in Jerusalem.

You are offered hospitality by members of the synagogue while you wait for the caravan master to get ready. He scurries from one end of the bazaar to the other, making deals and getting merchants to join the caravan. It takes several weeks to make all the preparations, but you only become more sure of what you want to do.

You take the caravan through Turkey, toward the Syrian coast and Palestine. One of the travelers lets you ride with him on his camel. Each day of the trip is full of new adventures. You huddle close to the campfire at night as you cross the Turkish mountains for it is cold. You also want to stay near the others because you've heard stories of bandits. Fortunately, nothing happens.

As you reach the blue Mediterranean shore, you see new sights: ruins of *Crusader* castles, orange trees, people in strange clothing. When you reach the *Holy Land*, you climb down from the camel and kiss the sacred soil.

Jews live in two cities, Jerusalem and Safed.

☞   *If you decide on Jerusalem,
turn to page 33.*

☞   *If you will live in Safed,
turn to page 34.*

19

The Catholic seminary is even stricter and more difficult than the boarding school. You have to get up before dawn to do your chores. Then you study and pray until late at night.

One day while you are sitting quietly thinking, you realize that you must make a decision. Do you want to continue and become a member of a religious order or will you leave and do something else?

☞   *If you continue your studies,*
    turn to page 35.

☞   *If you leave,*
    turn to page 36.

20

Military school is easier than the boarding school, and you do well. You seem to have a talent for artillery, so you are placed in charge of the garrison at the King's palace in Madrid. If the palace is attacked, your skill in using the large guns will be important.

In 1508, a rebellion breaks out among peasants on the border of Spain and Portugal. The King personally appoints you to be in charge of the troops who are sent to put down the rebellion. The army marches out to the sound of trumpets and drums.

You and your staff must decide whether to attack the rebels by sea or march across the land route.

☞   *If you go to Portugal by boat,*
      turn to page 37.

☞   *If you decide to go by land,*
      turn to page 38.

21

You return to your studies with even greater enthusiasm. You are determined to be such a good Catholic that no one will ever know of your Jewish past. Some of your friends think you're going too far; they call you "a fanatic."

You feel confused and angry whenever you remember the secret group of Jews in the cellar. You learn that they meet every week—on Friday afternoon. Should you tell the authorities that they are meeting there illegally? But some of them were your good friends. What shall you do?

☞   *If you report them,*
    turn to page 39.

☞   *If you keep silent,*
    turn to page 40.

22

Your decision puts you in a difficult position. Here you are, in a school which is training you to be a good Catholic, perhaps even a member of a religious order, and you're becoming convinced that you made a mistake. Now you think you should have left all your belongings and fled as a refugee. "I had a good life in Spain," you recall. "I could have started over elsewhere. At least I would have been a Jew in freedom."

You can think of only two possibilities. You can stay at the school, but try to practice some Jewish rituals secretly, or you can try to escape. Which do you choose?

☞　　*If you decide to stay,*
　　　turn to page 41.

☞　　*If you decide to escape,*
　　　turn to page 42.

23

The priest nods and leads you out of the room. "Don't waste your time with those books; they are full of mistakes. Let's go into the church and pray."

Later that day you receive a letter from the *Inquisition*. You are told to report to their headquarters at dawn the next day. The priest must have reported your secret reading.

☞ *If you go to headquarters as ordered,
turn to page 43.*

☞ *If you decide to run away,
turn to page 44.*

24

The priest knocks the book from your hand and kicks it across the room. "These books were hidden because they contain lies," he says. "People may only read books approved by the Church. That is the only way we can be sure that they learn the truth."

You are surprised. Then the priest grabs you by the shoulder and drags you out of the room. You try to tell him: "Father, I am trying to be a good Catholic. I was only curious about what the books were. I want to be a Catholic now."

He turns to you with contempt. "Once a Jew, always a Jew," he hisses at you. Maybe he's right.

☞   *If you stay with your studies,*
    turn to page 45.

☞   *If the priest is right and you decide to return to Judaism,*
    turn to page 46.

25

After several days of hiding during the day and walking at night, you arrive at the port city of Algeciras. You tell yourself the worst part of the ordeal is over. Now all you have to do is find a ship that's leaving Spain.

As you walk along the dock, you see a sailor and approach him: "Señor, I am looking for a job on a ship. Do you know anyone who might help me?" "Amigo," he replies, "you have come to the right person. I am from a ship that leaves today, and we need a worker like you."

You're not sure. He looks tough, maybe even evil. Yet he does have a ship.

☞ *If you decide to run from him,
    turn to page 47.*

☞ *If you sign on as a sailor,
    turn to page 48.*

26

You find yourself in a soft featherbed in the palace of a very rich Jew in the city of Venice. The room is full of dark carved wood furniture. Heavy draperies cover the windows and paintings of serious-faced people hang on the walls. As you peek out of the four-poster bed, you notice that angels fly over your head on the decorated ceiling. You can hardly believe your eyes. Who would think that any Jew could be so wealthy?

A servant enters, asks you to dress, and tells you that you are expected in the library. You enter the book-lined room to find a middle-aged gentleman. After he finds out who you are, he says: "I am *Joseph Nasi de Naxos.* Our family has ships and trades with countries all over Europe. For many years, I had business dealings with your father. He is an honorable and good man, and now I want to help you. I have been impressed with your courage and determination; it took great effort for you to reach Venice. You may have a job with us, either here or at our office in Turkey. Tell me tomorrow which you would prefer."

☞   *If you stay in Venice,
    turn to page 49.*

☞   *If you go to Turkey,
    turn to page 50.*

27

You find a deserted warehouse near the harbor with an office at the rear. With a little work, this area can be converted into living quarters, and no one will suspect that a Jew is illegally hiding there.

The alterations are made; you move in. Even though you think you are safe, you are afraid and still very careful. The *Inquisition* has spies everywhere.

One night you hear soldiers marching. They stop right outside the warehouse. Have you been discovered?

☞ *If you think the hideaway is still safe,
turn to page 51.*

☞ *If you decide to run away,
turn to page 52.*

28

You know that it would be fastest to follow the coastline directly east through San Sebastian and then to the French village of Biarritz. On the other hand, you also know that the *Inquisition* would expect fleeing Jews to do just that. Perhaps you ought to head inland and try to slip through a narrow mountain pass.

☞   *To follow the coastal route,*
     turn to page 53.

☞   *To go inland,*
     turn to page 54.

29

The ship docks in Nantes, a city with a long history of religious toleration. Merchants there have learned that fighting over religion is destructive and prevents them from making profits.

These men have made Nantes a very wealthy city with a bustling business district along the Loire River and impressive public and religious buildings. Because Jews seem to have a knack for commerce, they have been made welcome. A small but active Jewish community has been established. They have even plans to build a synagogue.

Some of the Jews of Nantes try to convince you to settle there; but you've heard of equally good reasons to go on to Amsterdam.

☞   *If you stay,*
    turn to page 55.

☞   *If you travel onward,*
    turn to page 56.

30

Fortunately, you managed to carry along a few gold coins.
You are able to bribe the Commandant of the port to let you
board one of the other ships now being loaded at the docks.
You must get away from Spain—almost anywhere would
be better than remaining in Spain. However, you remind
the Commandant that you have given him a good deal of
money and that you expect him to get you passage to some
place where Jews can live safely.

Late in the evening, he comes to your room and tells
you that two ships are ready. One goes north to several
ports, while the other is heading west to the New World.

☞   *If you still want to go to Holland,*
     turn to page 57.

☞   *If you want to take your chances in the New World,*
     turn to page 58.

31

You go with the merchant to his warehouse. You will begin to learn about his business. He specializes in the buying and selling of fine wines. You learn that the large barrels contain wine from Algeria; the smaller ones come from France and Italy; and the strangely-scented ones are filled with a Greek wine called retsina. Later, you discover that this wine gets its name from pine resin which flavors the new wine when it is stored in pine barrels. Tasting this strange wine and the more usual ones, you soon learn to distinguish which are good and valuable and which are worthless.

One day, your employer offers you a new opportunity. "You know enough now to act as my agent. How would you like to go to Algeria and buy some wine?"

☞ *If you agree to go,*
turn to page 59.

☞ *If you ask to be excused from the mission,*
turn to page 60.

32

You learn to sew. At first, you do basting, hemming, and buttonholes. After four years of working on your master's designs, you are allowed to select cloth and design your own elegantly-tailored garments. It has taken time to pass through the apprentice stage and become a master clothier. Yet a tailor's life is a satisfying type of life for you. As time passes, many rich and famous people ask you to design their clothes. You grow wealthy and are a respected member of the Jewish and Turkish communities.

One day a man knocks on your door. He introduces himself as Antonio de Salvo. You are surprised; Antonio was one of your childhood friends in Madrid, and now he is here looking like a prosperous businessman. You clap your hands, and a servant brings you cups of thick, sweet Turkish coffee.

After a while Antonio leans over toward you and whispers: "I've got a marvelous chance to make a lot of money, but I need some extra cash to start out. You'll triple your investment if only I can get my cargo of spices to France."

☞ If you remain a tailor,
turn to page 61.

☞ If you decide to lend Antonio the money,
turn to page 62.

33

The Jerusalem to which you come is a small city inhabited by Jews, Christians, and Moslems. It is hardly the city of *David* and *Solomon* you imagined from reading the *Bible*. Yet, as you look around, the stones remind you of the city's former greatness and of God's Temple, the western wall of which you can still see.

You move in with a Jewish family and try to decide what to do. Finally, you commit yourself to becoming a scholar. You want to learn as much as you can about the history of Jerusalem.

☞　　*Turn to page 63.*

34

Safed is becoming a city of mystics. Jews who live there study the *Kabbalah*, the treasure-house of mystical ideas, miracles, and wisdom. You join the circle of scholars who are permitted to study; not everyone receives such permission because legend has it that too much knowledge of the *Kabbalah* can be dangerous. You may lose your mind.

Every day you and the other students join the circle of *Joseph Karo* and *Solomon Alkabetz* to pore through the *Zohar*, the mystical book of splendor, learning the secrets of the universe. You wonder how the world came into being, what God looks like, and how to bring the *Messiah*.

One day, as you are immersed in study, you feel a force pushing against you. You see nothing, but the sensation of pressure is very real. You wonder whether you have gone too far, whether you should pull back?

☞ *If you decide to give up studying the Kabbalah, turn to page 109.*

☞ *If you continue to study in Safed, turn to page 107.*

35

When you graduate and become ordained, you are assigned to a church in Pamplona near the Pyrénées Mountains. The people seem happy with you, and you feel completely at home.

One day a family of Jewish refugees knocks on your door. "We are fleeing from the *Inquisition*, trying to get across the mountains to safety. Some of us remember your father and know that you were born a Jew. Please help us get past the border guards."

What will you do? If you help them, you may be exposed as a friend of the Jews and perhaps you too will have to flee. On the other hand, if you denounce them, you know that they will be arrested.

☞ *If you decide to help,*
turn to page 64.

☞ *If you decide to turn them in to the police,*
turn to page 65.

36

Once outside the seminary gates, you've no idea where to go. You've been trained to be a religious member of the Church; that won't help you now.

Suddenly, you have an idea. You remember that your father knew Don Luis Garcia y Vega, a prominent and wealthy merchant. Perhaps he can help.

Don Luis greets you warmly and makes two suggestions: "I have a shop in Toledo which needs a trustworthy manager; you could handle it easily. I'm also sending out an expedition to the New World. Sail with it if you want, and you can look out for my interests."

☞   *If you decide to set up shop in Toledo,*
    turn to page 66.

☞   *If you go to the New World,*
    turn to page 67.

37

When you get to the port city of Cadiz, you are disappointed to discover that no one ordered the navy to meet you there. Without boats, you cannot proceed. You send your fastest rider back to Madrid for instructions.

He returns in a few days, but not alone. With him is a new commanding officer to take your place. Even though it was not your fault, you are blamed for what has happened. In disgrace, you are taken back to the capital and placed in a dungeon. Sitting chained in the cell, you wonder if you would have been treated so harshly if your parents had not been Jewish. You don't have a long time to worry about this question. After a quick trial, you are executed.

END

38

After a hard, seven-day march from Madrid, you attack in force at Badajoz. Your seasoned soldiers are able to defeat the peasants and the local militia. Your army pushes well into Portugal and captures all the rebels. Now you must decide whether to send everyone home or to punish the leaders of the rebellion.

    If you send them home,
        turn to page 68.

    If you decide on punishment,
        turn to page 69.

39

The priest in charge of the boarding school is astounded. "What, a secret group of Jews here in the boarding school!" Later that evening, as you lead some soldiers to the cellar room, you hear the chanting of Hebrew prayers. "See," you say, "I told you so!"

The secret Jews are captured and imprisoned. A special court of the *Inquisition* decides their future. Because of your evidence, they are condemned to be burned at the stake in an *auto-da-fé*. You are left with painful, mixed feelings. Did you do your duty . . . or did you betray your friends?

☞ *If you feel satisfied that you did your duty,*
   turn to page 70.

☞ *If you grieve because you betrayed your friends,*
   turn to page 71.

40

In time, your studies absorb you completely, and your anger passes. After you graduate from the boarding school, you go on to the seminary. Then you are assigned to assist the Spanish Cardinal who lives in Rome. It is a great honor for someone as young as you. Quickly, you pack your trunk and make plans to travel to your new post.

Some of your friends suggest you go by horse-drawn coach through southern France and northern Italy. Others recommend a sea trip from Valencia to Naples and then overland to Rome. Which one do you select?

☞　　*If you go by land,*
　　　turn to page 72.

☞　　*If you go by sea,*
　　　turn to page 73.

41

You decide to become a *Marrano*, a secret Jew. But it's not easy in a Catholic school. You try to avoid eating pork, but it's hard to avoid suspicion. On Friday night, you sneak away to light *Shabbat* candles in a secret room, and, even though you have no Jewish calendar, quietly you recite the prayers you remember on days you think are Jewish holy days.

One Friday night, one of your fellow students follows you. He sees what you are doing and immediately turns you in to the authorities. You are arrested and convicted of practicing Judaism while pretending to be a Catholic. You are sentenced to death and burned at the stake during a public *auto-da-fé* in the town square.

E N D

42

You make your plans carefully. Any one of your classmates
could be a spy for the *Inquisition*. A warm coat is hidden
at the bottom of your locker. Extra scraps of food fill the
pockets of every garment. Now all you can do is wait . . .
wait for a dark night with no moon.

Finally, the time comes. You wait until everyone else is
asleep, and then you grab your coat and a few of your most-
prized possessions and steal out of the dormitory.

When you reach the gate, you are surprised to see a
nightwatchman. This is something you did not consider in
your plans. You think quickly. Should you take the
underground tunnel out of the school or should you go
around the building and climb over the wall?

☞   *If you decide to crawl through the tunnel,*
      turn to page 74.

☞   *If you decide to go over the wall,*
      turn to page 75.

43

You are terrified as you arrive at *Inquisition* headquarters. You show your letter and are led into a small room. No one else is there. You wait for hours. Finally, a guard comes and tells you to follow him. He takes you to a larger room where seven men are seated behind a table. They look like judges.

"Sit down! We want only to ask you a few questions." They ask you why you chose to stay in Spain and to become a convert. They also want to know about your studies and about your day-to-day life. You answer truthfully and in a strong voice. When the session is over, you are told to wait in the same small room.

☞ If you think you convinced them that you are sincere, turn to page 76.

☞ If you think they are suspicious, turn to page 77.

44

You were able to get out of Madrid without being stopped. You have been on the run for a while. You're tired. But you cannot rest. You must keep going! The mountains already seem close enough to touch. Another day or so, and you'll be safely across them. There, you will find other Jews. They'll take care of you.

At nightfall, you come to a small farmhouse. You haven't eaten all day so you take a chance and knock on the door. The farmer and his wife are kind. They give you food and invite you to spend the night. A soft bed sounds great, but the mountains are your real goal.

☞   *If you stay,*
turn to page 78.

☞   *If you continue walking,*
turn to page 79.

45

You are given extra fast days and tedious study assignments to make up for your sins. You are tired and hungry most of the time, but you bear up and do your work well. Your teachers are pleased. Finally, the day comes. You are paraded to the Cathedral with the other students. The service is long and solemn with music and prayers in Latin.

Cardinal dos Passos calls you to the altar one by one. "Are you certain that you want to be a Catholic? Do you give up any attachment to the dead faith of Judaism and swear total allegiance to the Holy Catholic Church?" he asks. "Yes, Your Eminence," you reply. "Then I declare that you and all your friends are *Conversos* and that you are now Catholics."

Bells ring; everyone is happy; it's a great day.

E N D

46

That night you decide to make your move. You wait until everyone is asleep—and then you wait a bit longer. Finally, you dress quietly and slip out of the school. By morning you are on your way to the Mediterranean coast. There, you have heard, people will help you.

When you arrive at the city of Zaragoza, you find a fork in the road. One leads directly northeast over the mountains, while the other continues toward the east and the city of Barcelona. As a fugitive, you cannot even ask anyone's advice. Which will you take?

☞ *If you decide to head northeast,*
  turn to page 80.

☞ *If you continue east,*
  turn to page 81.

47

As you start to run down the street, a group of soldiers on horseback rides around the corner. There is nowhere to run. The *Inquisition* in front and the sailor behind make escape seem impossible.

Suddenly, a hand reaches out from a doorway and pulls you in. You start to scream, but a kindly looking gentleman places his finger to his lips and says: "Silencio." You obey.

Later, after a good meal, you learn that your host, Don Diego, was once Jewish himself. He understands your situation and promises to help. In the middle of the night, he wakes you up. "It's time to go. The tide is right, and the ship is about to leave. Hurry." You thank him with tears in your eyes.

After the ship leaves the harbor and sets sail for the east, you ask one of the officers, "Where are we headed?" "Don't you know? Palestine!"

As you reach the sandy shore of Palestine, you see new sights: ruins of the *Crusader* castle at *Caesarea*, orange trees, people in strange clothing. A small boat comes out to your anchored ship. Dark-skinned men row you and the others to the beach. You leap into the gentle surf and race up onto the beach. This is the *Holy Land!* You fling yourself forward and kiss the sacred soil.

Jews live in two cities, Jerusalem and Safed.

☞   *If you decide on Jerusalem,*
     turn to page 33.

☞   *If you will live in Safed,*
     turn to page 34.

48

Your worst fears were true. As you walk beside him, the sailor grabs your arm and drags you to a filthy ship. Soon, you find yourself serving as a slave on a ship of the terrible *Barbary Pirates*, headed for Tunis.

One morning you wake up and hear a loud voice. A Venetian trading ship has been sighted. What a prize! Oh, no! What a surprise! The trading ship turns out to be a corsair, a very fast fighting ship used to protect slower merchant ships from attacking pirates. Your ship is trapped. The fight is fierce. The pirates are overpowered; sailors from the corsair board your ship. As the Venetian sailor comes to capture you, you move to the side of the ship. Now you are faced with a choice. Do you jump overboard or do you allow yourself to be captured and placed in irons?

☞ *If you jump,*
turn to page 82.

☞ *If you allow yourself to be captured,*
turn to page 83.

49

You are assigned to *Joseph Nasi de Naxos*'s counting house. The work is not hard. You learn quickly and are promoted. Pretty soon, you are in charge of the office.

One day, *Señor de Naxos* himself comes to your office and tells you that he has something important to discuss with you. "You've done very well," he says. "I'm proud of you. But as the *Torah* says, 'It is not good for a man or woman to be alone.' Therefore, I've arranged for you to marry into a prominent family. Come to my palace tonight. Your intended will be there."

"Can this be true?" you wonder. "I am just a poor refugee. Now *Señor de Naxos* has arranged a very fine marriage for me." It's hard to believe, but it is true.

With a family like that and a friend like *Señor de Naxos*, your future can only be happy.

END

50

You leave Venice at dusk and sail down the Adriatic Sea. After stopping at Bari, the ship heads through the Peloponnesus and docks at Constantinople.

You spend the next six years as an apprentice in one of *Joseph Nasi de Naxos*'s stores, learning all about the business. Finally, you are ready to be on your own. You set up your office quickly and begin to follow the trading orders you receive from Venice. Buy a little olive oil, sell some cloth. So it goes. Slowly, you are getting rich.

One day, a beggar comes to your door. It is a *mitzvah* never to turn a poor person away; so you give him a few coins. He hands you a note: "A golden opportunity awaits you in the east. Form a caravan at once." The note is not signed. You dismiss the thought from your mind as ridiculous . . . but then you wonder. What new adventure has life offered you?

☞   *If you decide to gamble on the note,*
       turn to page 86.

☞   *If you play it safe,*
       turn to page 87.

51

After an anxious half-hour, the soldiers leave. You look out the window and, from the orange peels in the gutter, you decide they just stopped for a snack. What a relief!

Another week passes, and the Cardinal's ship is ready. He sends a message that you should come to the dock at midnight. The guard has been bribed to let you aboard.

When you arrive at the dock, however, there are two ships ready to depart, and you're not sure which one belongs to the Cardinal.

☞   *If you choose a ship called the Santa Caterina,
     turn to page 89.*

☞   *If you try to board the Muerte (Death),
     turn to page 90.*

52

Quickly, you gather a few things and prepare to dash out the back door. Meanwhile, the soldiers you fear have been having a snack of oranges. They weren't looking for you at all, but you don't know it.

The sergeant tells them to get ready to move on, but some of them have to go to the bathroom. "Go around the back of the warehouse," the sergeant says. "No one will see you."

You don't see them, either. As you dash out, they are standing right there, and you are captured at once. What rotten luck! The soldiers think you are a heretic, a Jew who converts to Catholicism and then begins to live Jewishly again. That definitely violates the laws of the *Inquisition*. You are placed in chains and dragged off to prison.

☞   *Turn to page 77.*

53

Cardinal de Sourdes has given you the letter of protection and the *snuffbox* which you place in a very safe place. If you need them, you want them to be available.

Disguised as a peasant, you start out toward France. The day is beautiful with a bright blue sky and deep blue sea. You're glad to be alive, and you start to sing aloud. Suddenly you stop . . . terrified . . . frightened. You realize that you were singing a Jewish folk song with Hebrew lyrics.

☞   *Turn to page 88.*

54

The Pyrénées are not high mountains, but they are very rugged. Traveling through them will be difficult and tiring. You know that robbers and bandits hide in the mountain passes.

When you reach the foothills, you notice a change in the people. These are *Basques,* ferocious fighters and very independent. No one tells them what to do!

A *Basque* chieftain comes up to you: "You are a Jew. We have heard that the *Inquisition* has expelled you. No one should be able to do that, even to Jews. We'll protect you through the mountains."

☞ *If you trust him and accept his protection,*
turn to page 93.

☞ *If you decide to go by yourself,*
turn to page 94.

55

You settle in Nantes on the banks of the Loire River and begin a small trading business of your own. Every tide brings in new ships, and you always seem to find something to buy or sell. One day, a sinister looking man with a crescent-shaped scar on his cheek strides into your shop and holds out a chest of precious silverware. From his looks, you suspect he is a pirate, and you're convinced when you examine the goods that they're stolen! He appears to be ferocious, and you are frightened. He demands money for the chest and leaves saying he will be back.

Later that day, the Duke, Jean le Bonhomme, sends his police through the trading district. They inquire about a pirate with stolen goods. You are afraid. What if you are found out?

☞   *If you decide to risk staying in Nantes, turn to page 95.*

☞   *If you think it would be safer in Holland, turn to page 96.*

☞   *If you decide the right thing to do is to inform the police, turn to page 110.*

56

Leaving Nantes, you travel slowly up the Loire Valley past beautiful castles under the shadow of the cathedral at Orleans and into the village of Versailles. Paris is not too far now, only a few miles away.

It's Friday afternoon, *erev Shabbat.* You stop at a tavern to clean up and observe the day of rest. When you sit down to eat, three rough men come up to you. They punch you in the face and steal your money. As they ride off you overhear: "Those Jews! Who do they think they are? We'll teach them a lesson. Besides, it's their Sabbath and they can't even fight back."

After *Havdalah,* you leave Versailles and, penniless, continue your journey toward Holland.

☞   *Turn to page 96.*

57

The ship's first stop is the English port of Rye. You sit
on deck and watch the hustle and bustle on the docks.
Everyone is trading, loading, buying, or selling. Such a
commotion!

A dark man comes aboard. After a few private words
with the Captain, he turns to you. *"Shalom!* My name is
David Nieto. A few of us have settled here, despite the desire
of *King Henry VII* to keep England free of Jews, like his
ally Spain. We've already established a small Jewish
community. We follow our Jewish practices very quietly,
privately, but at least we manage. Please come ashore and
join us."

☞ *If you decide to stay in Rye,*
turn to page 97.

☞ *If you remain on the same ship,*
turn to page 98.

☞ *If you disembark, but leave on another ship,*
turn to page 99.

58

Your ship docks at a beautiful island and you go ashore.
Brilliantly-colored birds call from tall palm trees as the
gentle sea curls on a white sand beach. You look around;
this must be paradise.

Life on the island, however, is not ideal. No farms have
been planted, so you must live on roots, berries, fruit, and
coconuts. Sometimes you are able to catch small animals
and fish. The huts you occupy leak during tropical storms,
and your fellow Europeans very often fall sick.

One day, a ship stops on its way west toward Peru. You
wonder if you should join them.

☞   If you remain on the island,
      turn to page 100.

☞   If you move on,
      turn to page 101.

59

Your Algeria-bound ship sails from Constantinople, but a storm rises in the Aegean Sea. Near the island of Skiros, the ship runs aground, and everyone aboard is tossed into the sea. Through great luck, you grab a piece of wood and float ashore.

Lying on the beach, trying to catch your breath, you see some rough-looking men approach. They are pirates. "Ah, a survivor," one says menacingly. He tells the others they should throw you back into the sea. "No," says the Captain. "We can use another hand on board." They drag you to their ship.

You resign yourself to life on a pirate ship. Compared to drowning, it doesn't seem so terrible.

END

60

You remain in Constantinople and decide to learn about the wine business. Your employer gives you a job checking the casks; later, you are promoted and given the responsibility of supervising the ordering and shipping of all the merchandise. Soon you are transferred to another department where you learn how to take care of the financial side of the business.

One day, your employer takes you aside. "You have come a long way from the refugee I took in seven years ago. Now, you are ready to join me as a partner. I am growing older; you are still young and vigorous. Someday, you will own this business and be very wealthy. Be careful! Learn how to use wisely your wealth and power. Always remember that whatever you have is given you by God. You should share what you have with others. *Tsedakah* is the Jewish way."

You listen well and take what he says to heart. His teachings become guidelines for your life.

☞ *Turn to page 84.*

61

Your reputation as a fine tailor spreads throughout Europe. Traders for the *de Naxos* family travel through a huge international empire of commerce, reaching from Holland to Persia and many places in between. Everywhere, they mention your name.

One day, a messenger brings a letter sealed with wax and fancy ribbon. "His Royal Highness, the King of France, having heard of your fame as a tailor, will graciously allow you to enter his court as Royal Tailor. Your presence is commanded."

☞   *If you decide that Turkey is now your home,*
turn to page 85.

☞   *If you decide to go to France,*
turn to page 104.

62

You should have investigated Antonio more carefully. Unfortunately for you, he turned out to be dishonest and ran off with your money. Not only that, but he also left you as his partner responsible for all his bills. Soon his creditors come to collect. Your merchandise is sold to pay Antonio's debts, and you have little more than the clothes on your back. Now, you are bankrupt.

"Well," you think, "that's how I started out. I can do it again." And you start out a second time to make your fortune.

E N D

63

You study the *Bible,* *Talmud,* and *Midrash* and make notes about every mention of Jerusalem. During the morning hours, you walk through the city and become so familiar with it that you feel personally related to every building. After many years, you become known as the most learned scholar of Jerusalem's history.

Now you must make a choice. How will you use all this knowledge? Some urge you to stay in Jerusalem to greet dignitaries. Others suggest you travel to teach many people.

☞   *If you remain in Jerusalem,*
      turn to page 105.

☞   *If you decide to go abroad,*
      turn to page 106.

64

"Come with me," you say. "I shall see that you get safely into France."

Late that night, you walk up to the border and start to talk to the guard. While you are talking, the Jewish family slips past the border and into friendly territory.

You return to the church. What you did was illegal, but you feel good; it was the right thing to do, even if it meant risking your own safety. You remember your Jewish roots and know that you had to help the refugees.

Years pass. No one ever finds out. You live in peace.

END

65

"Stay in the cellar until nightfall," you say. "I'll see what I can do."

You hurry to the center of town and listen for rumors in the marketplace. People whisper about some Jewish refugees who are supposed to be nearby. A shudder of fear passes through your body.

"It's too dangerous," you say to yourself. "I must turn them over to the police. Otherwise, I'll be discovered and punished by the *Inquisition*."

When the authorities come to arrest the Jews, they arrest you, too! "You were once a Jew," they say. "You must still be a secret Jew, a *Marrano*. That's why these people came to you." As you march off to prison and probable death, you are angry and confused. But nothing can help you now.

END

66

The shop is small, but it does well under your management. You soon buy other businesses. You become wealthy, marry, and raise five children. Life seems kind to you.

One day, you are called before the *Inquisition*. They accuse you of escaping from the seminary many years ago and of secretly practicing Judaism. You deny their charges but are condemned. You and your family are paraded to the central square of the city and shamed. After you publicly confess your sins, your property is taken away from you, and you are forced to spend your life serving others. As you and your family live out your days in poverty, you wonder: "Did I really make a wise decision, after all?"

END

67

As you cross the Atlantic Ocean, the seas are calm. But, near Hispaniola, a storm comes up, and the ship is wrecked on an island. You and six others are the only survivors.

The island is not deserted. Hostile natives creep up to your camp while you sleep and capture all of you. They take you back to their village. As you enter the village, you realize that these natives are cannibals. You try to run, but it's too late. A poison dart enters your shoulder, and you fall to the ground.

END

68

As the people go home, you start a conversation with a gentleman from Portugal. He tells you that there is still a large secret Jewish population in that country and that Jews can still manage to practice their religion.

His words stir some long-hidden feelings in you. It has been sixteen years since you last thought of yourself as a Jew. But, once the idea creeps into your mind, you cannot escape it. "You are a Jew; you are a Jew."

That night, you leave your tent on the battlefield and walk outside to look at the starry sky. Something—you can't describe it—forces you onward. Soon you are striding toward the small town of Evora. At dawn, you stand outside the secret synagogue. Morning prayers are about to begin. You enter. As the *chazan* begins to chant very softly, you feel tears on your cheeks. You realize this is where you belong, among fellow Jews.

END

69

You take the leaders as prisoners and march back to the capital. All along the road, people cheer and throw flowers. When you return and report to *King Ferdinand*, he receives you warmly and gives you a special medal. You are named Commandant of the Garrison of Madrid. You marry and live the rest of your life in comfort with riches and honor.

END

70

As time goes on, you become known as a great defender of the Catholic faith. The *Inquisition* appoints you "Special Inquisitor for the Jews," and you spend the next years hunting down groups of secret Jews. You are known to be merciless. Even Catholics who do not eat pork are suspected. You become very wealthy because you receive a share of the money confiscated from each convicted *Judaizer.* Finally, you are one of the most powerful people in Spain.

As you straighten your velvet robe and lean back in your chair, you smile and look around your palatial apartment. Just today, you have condemned a family of five to the *auto-da-fé.*

END

71

You feel very guilty. These friends of yours never did anything wrong. They never hurt you. Why should they be punished just because they are Jews? You feel it is not too late and you must help them.

Silently, you enter the prison tower and sneak up on the guard. When he is not watching, you take a broom handle and hit him hard on his head. He falls unconscious at your feet. Quickly, you unlock the cells and lead your friends outside.

"Here," you say, "take this paper with you. It is a passport which will help get you over the Pyrénées and into France. There you will be safe. Go now! Hurry before anyone sees you!"

After they have gone, you consider your own future. You decide that you have already made a commitment to be a Catholic, but something went wrong. Maybe the Church was the wrong choice. You should have selected to be an officer in the King's army.

☞   *Turn to page 20.*

72

As you cross the Pyrénées and enter France, you find many Jews who had been expelled from Spain. They have settled in towns along the Mediterranean coast.

You meet one of their rabbis and challenge him to a debate: "Which is the true religion, Catholicism or Judaism?" At the end of the debate, neither of you has convinced the other. But you are impressed with the rabbi and his deep knowledge. Not only does he know about Judaism, but also he can speak of philosophy, medicine, astronomy, and mathematics.

In Rome, you remember this man. One thing he said, in particular, stays with you. "I know we shall never agree. You believe you are right, while I think that Judaism is true. Isn't it possible for us to disagree and still respect each other?"

END

73

The sea voyage begins with rough seas. Then, the weather clears, and you are able to go on deck.

A member of the *Inquisition* is traveling with you. He takes you into his confidence. "Now that we've finally gotten rid of the Spanish Jews, we've got to pursue the *Conversos*. Even though the *Inquisition* has been interested in them for a few years, we've got to try harder. You know," he leans over toward you with a conspiratorial look, "there are a lot of people who think the Jews converted to save their souls. We know better. All they wanted to do was save their money and social position. Well, we have a surprise for them. After the *Inquisition* tries them as heretics, their wealth will belong to us!"

Your first impulse is to argue with him. You feel your heart pounding and your face flushing. But, then, you think to yourself: "I'm a good Catholic. There's nothing Jewish about me any longer. But this fellow will never understand. I had better keep quiet."

You just nod and excuse yourself. For the rest of the trip, you stay far away from the member of the *Inquisition*. When the ship docks at Naples, you are relieved to find that he is not going to Rome. You hope you'll never see him again!

END

74

It's dark and slippery in the tunnel, so you crawl along, hoping your guesses are correct. Ahead you see a light. Perhaps it is the end of the tunnel.

As quietly as possible, you edge your way toward the light. It comes from a barred window at waist height. Through the window, you see some kind of cellar. You pull off one of the wooden bars and ease yourself up through the opening onto the stone floor. On the other side of the cellar is a worn stairway.

Carefully, you go up the stairs and enter a large room. Suddenly, you recognize the place. You have gone in a full circle. It is the dormitory hall of your school. What a shock! With tears in your eyes, you find your way back to bed and try to sleep.

☞   *Turn to page 41.*

75

The wall is about ten feet tall. Even though you are in excellent condition, you are still too short to climb it by yourself. There doesn't seem to be any way to scale the barrier.

Suddenly, you remember that the priests made wine from their own grapes. Grapes grow on vines, and vines are good for climbing. You grope along the wall until you come to the grape arbor. Its latticework is just as good as a ladder. You climb quickly. With this help, it's not difficult to climb the wall and slip quietly down the other side. You wait a moment. No sound. The watchman did not see you.

The road leads straight toward the mountains. You start walking. Soon it is dawn, and you are able to hitch a ride on a farmer's cart. You fall asleep as the cart bumps along. After a while, the farmer shakes you and says: "This is as far as we go."

☞   *Turn to page 44.*

76

You are led into the private suite of the *Grand Inquisitor.*
"We had been told that you are very bright and capable," he
says. "You proved that during the interview. We want you
to become a page in the royal court. Your duties will be to
assist us and the royal family with errands and other small
jobs. You will also attend a special school for especially-
talented children. When you graduate, you will receive an
important position."

You feel numb with gratitude and fall to your knees
before him. He holds out his right hand, and you kiss his
ring.

END

77

Two guards come in and drag you through the corridor and down several flights of stairs. An iron door is unlocked, and you are thrown into a large room. You cannot believe your eyes. The room is full of terrible machines; it is a torture chamber.

The *Grand Inquisitor* appears and tells you that they believe you are a secret Jew. You try to tell them that it isn't true, but no one listens. They strap you on a rack designed to tear your arms and legs from your body. Wheels turn; you hear yourself scream; the pain is unbearable. "Confess!" the *Inquisitor* screams at you. "We already know you are a *Marrano*. All you need to do is to tell us the names of your friends."

Just before you lose consciousness, you look at the *Inquisitor*. "*Shema Yisrael*," you say, "*Adonai . . . Elohenu . . . Adonai . . . Echad.*"

END

78

It's hard to resist the warm fire, good food, and soft bed. For the last three days, you have been traveling by night and hiding by day. This careful plan has kept you out of the clutches of the *Inquisition,* but you are so tired. . . .

Twenty-four hours later, the farmer awakens you. You can hardly believe that the hay-stuffed mattress has been your haven for all night and a full day. Now, he tells you that it is time to go.

"How can I go now?" you ask. "It's raining and the mountain trails are dangerous at night." But he assures you that everything will work out. He gives you food and water and points you toward a distant light. "At that farmhouse, they will give you additional directions. Don't worry!"

You thank him warmly and step outside. Heading toward France, your ears ring with his final farewell: "God be with you!"

☞ *Turn to page 54.*

79

"I'm tired, and I'm grateful to you. I wish I could stay, but I've got to keep going toward the mountains."

The farmer understands and gives you some food. His wife draws the curtains to hide your presence, but she seems to have trouble. The curtains flutter back and forth several times until they close completely.

You thank your hosts warmly and step outside . . . into the arms of a waiting squad of soldiers. The Lieutenant turns to your hosts and tosses them a bag of coins: "The King and the *Inquisition* are grateful that you signaled us."

You realize the fluttering of the curtains gave you away.

It's over. You return to Madrid in chains.

END

80

After a month of wandering through the Pyrénées and along the French part of the Mediterranean coast, you spend a few days resting in the Italian city of Genoa. Finally, you move on to the small town of Soncino. The Jews who moved there from Spain have started a fine printing press, and you find a job helping to print Jewish books.

One day, while you are binding a set of the *Talmud* with fine leather, you break into uncontrollable laughter. Everyone gathers around, so you tell them the story. "When I was in Madrid, studying to be a Catholic, I got into trouble reading Jewish books. That's why I ran and ended up being Jewish instead of Catholic. So where do I spend my days, breaking my fingers and straining my back? Making Jewish books!"

E N D

81

You arrive at the port of Barcelona and manage to stow away on a trading ship. During a stop in Marseilles, you jump ashore. You hope there is a Jewish community in this city.

You look for a building that might be a synagogue. If you can find one, you'll meet Jews at *shacharit*. It's not hard. The big *Star of David* gives it away. You walk in, cover your head, and enter the sanctuary. You are home.

END

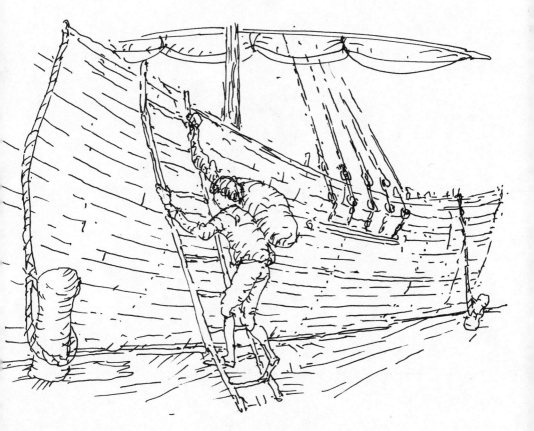

82

You hit your arm against the side of the ship as you jump, and your shoulder aches with terrible pain. You search for a piece of driftwood, but you can't find one. Jumping was a mistake. You struggle to stay afloat, but it's a losing battle. You slip beneath the cold, dark water and drown.

END

83

The Venetian corsair which has captured you puts in at
Venice. You and the pirate crew are sent to prison. In the
dungeon, the *Barbary Coast* pirates plead to *Allah* for help.
You feel like praying yourself—but how? Are you still a Jew,
or are you now a Catholic?

You can't decide. The pirates all around you seem so
sure of their faith. Suddenly, you find yourself reciting
"Shema Yisrael. . . ." As you chant, a jailer unlocks your
chains and leads you out of the dungeon. He takes you up
a flight of steps to a wide hall where you see a richly-
dressed man.

"So this is the Jewish sailor among the pirates." He
says you look healthy enough and orders the guards to
bring you to his palace.

From the filthy, rat-infested dungeon, you are placed in
a horse-drawn carriage and driven across the city.

☞   *Turn to page 26.*

84

You continue in business. When you reach the age of twenty-three, you marry and begin your family. Two sons and a daughter soon sit around the family table. You have gained the reputation of total honesty, and people respect you.

When your daughter reaches the age of eighteen, you arrange a good marriage for her. She is beautiful, talented, and has a substantial dowry. You look for a suitable young man.

The *de Naxos* family has a son named Joseph who will someday be head of the *de Naxos* business empire. You hesitate. Would the daughter of a Spanish Jewish refugee be acceptable? Then you remember that the aristocratic *de Naxos* family also fled from Spain.

You approach *Señor de Naxos* and, to your surprise, he agrees. The young couple will be married soon, just before *Pesach*. Only one problem remains. Where will the wedding ceremony be held?

☞　　*If it will be at the de Naxos palace,*
　　　turn to page 102.

☞　　*If your home will be the place,*
　　　turn to page 103.

85

Saying "no" to a king is dangerous. The *Sultan* calls you in to discuss your decision. "If you can refuse the King of France, you might try to refuse me as well. So that you learn this lesson well, you shall spend the next month as my guest—in prison!"

At the end of an unpleasant month, you are released and returned to your business and family. You appreciate the luxury of your life in Turkey, but you know now that the *Sultan* can expel you as easily as did *Ferdinand* and *Isabella*. Jewish life is still uncertain, but you reason it is probably just as uncertain in every other country. So you decide to remain in Turkey.

END

86

Sometimes, a gamble is worthwhile. You invest in a caravan that will be gone for nearly two years. When it returns, each animal is heavily loaded with treasures.

"You see," says the caravan leader, "when we reached the province of *Sinkiang*, we met a community of strange people. Their Chinese name means 'People who do not eat pork.' They live in the town of *Kai-Feng-Fu*, and they helped us make excellent trades."

After he leaves, you laugh for a long time. "When I was young," you think, "my people were expelled from our homeland in Spain—and now I find that I have Jewish relatives all over the world!"

END

87

Buying and selling all sorts of goods produces a comfortable life for you and your family. Everyone in the community respects you and, as you grow older, people ask your advice. You are elected *parnas* of your synagogue and sit in an honored place at services. You are content that your life has been worthwhile and that you have made good choices throughout all your adventures.

END

88

You look around. It wasn't a very smart thing to do. What if someone heard you singing a forbidden Jewish song?

As you stop for a meal, your worst fears are confirmed. The peasant with the cart next to you says to his wife and daughter: "Did you hear that stranger singing a Jewish song?"

Your first thought is to get out of there as fast as possible. You think again. To run would give everything away; maybe you should ignore him and stick to your original plans.

☞   *If you decide to flee,*
      turn to page 91.

☞   *If you stay,*
      turn to page 92.

89

As you step on the gangplank of the Santa Caterina, the watchman bows low: "We've been expecting you." And so they have—the *Inquisition*, that is. *De Sourdes* has set a trap, and you walked right into it.

You are marched off to prison surrounded by five soldiers. At your trial, you are accused of trying to smuggle gold coins out of the country and of leading good Catholics to sin by bribing them. The judges read you the charges, but every time you begin to speak in your own behalf you are forcibly silenced. The verdict has, apparently, been decided in advance. After the trial, you are taken to a public square and executed.

END

90

Nobody but a cardinal, you decide, would dare to name a ship Muerte. Trembling with fear, you climb the ramp. But it is a good choice, and soon you are securely settled in your cabin.

With the morning tide, the ship slips away from the dock and out of the harbor. Now, it's safe to appear on deck and say goodbye to Spain forever. In a few days, the ship will land at Nantes.

☞ *Turn to page 29.*

91

As you escape, you reconsider your original decision. Is it really so important to remain Jewish, especially when so much, even your life, is at stake? Would it be so terrible to be a Catholic?

You decide to head back toward Madrid. You've made a firm decision to convert.

☞   *Turn to page 11.*

92

The man approaches you. "Buenos dias, Señor," you say. It takes all your courage to keep calm on the surface. Then a surprise. "*Shalom*," he says in response to your greeting.

Shalom? He's a Jew like yourself! You discover that this is the *Aboab* family from *Castile*, trying to escape just as you are. You travel on together, more secure knowing that you're among friends.

Approaching the border guards, you produce the Cardinal's letter, and they let you through without any argument. Everyone is happy to be in France.

END

93

The *Basque* chieftain takes you up the side of a narrow valley and along a cliffside path. You look down; it's a long, sheer drop. The chieftain tells you that this route has been known to the *Basques* since the days of *Roland*, many years ago.

As you reach the French border, your *Basque* friends leave you with many gifts: a goatskin container of wine, some fresh bread, cheese, and Valencia oranges. "My friend," they say, "go with God." You thank them with all your heart, and tell them that this is precisely your intention. "I was expelled from Spain because of my religion; I will certainly be loyal to it now."

END

94

Going on alone doesn't seem so tough. At first, you are a bit scared as you travel the mountain road in the company of shepherds and other travelers. After a while, it seems safe. You let down your guard and begin to talk with the others. You even whistle a tune as you head over the crest and down the other side toward Perpignan.

Entering the town, you come across a group of *Dominican monks*. They stop you and ask you if you are a Spaniard. You are convinced that you are now safe, but you still hesitate to admit who you are. Just then, the fringe of your *talit katan* escapes from the bundle of clothing you carry. The monks surround you and beat you bloody. Just before you pass out on the ground, you hear them say: "Jew pig! Too many coming over the mountains like this one!"

You faint, but at least you are in France . . . free.

END

95

The next day, you hear the pirate was killed in a sword fight. To conceal the evidence, you melt down the silver into bars. It still sells for a good profit.

Together with your fellow Jews, you send a petition to the Duke. You want permission to build a synagogue. He answers: "Jewish subjects! The peace of the city may be disrupted if an alien house of prayer is erected. Worship your God, but be sure to follow your practices in private."

You are disappointed, but at least the Duke has given you permission to be Jewish. Most rulers in Europe wouldn't even agree to that. A room in your neighbor's store is used as the synagogue, and you are elected to the *Ajunto.*

You want to express your gratitude to God for your safe escape from Spain and your comfortable new life. With some of the money you got when you sold the pirate's silver, you establish the *Chevrah Gemilut Chasadim,* the "Jewish Aid Society." "No Jew will ever come to Nantes and be refused *tsedakah,*" you say. "We shall always be able to take care of our own poor people."

END

96

Holland seems to be the European country most hospitable to Jews, but, to get there, you must cross lands held by Spanish troops. There's no alternative.

You travel at night, keeping away from main roads, and hide during the day. You cannot trust anyone, so you steal food and sometimes go hungry.

When you reach the Belgian city of Antwerp, you realize that you have only a few miles to go. You're so impatient that you leave your hiding place before dark. Spanish cavalry spots you and gives chase. You run as fast as possible, but it's gaining. Suddenly, you come to a wide canal. You dive in. Thank goodness your father knew that the *Talmud* required him to teach you to swim. The cavalry stops at the edge of the canal, yells insults, and then turns back. You are safe!

As you dry off in Holland, you praise God for your escape and for leading you to a land where you can be a Jew.

END

97

Of course, it's no secret that there are Jews living in England illegally. Even *King Henry VII* knows. But there are only a few. They are good traders. England wants to become wealthy.

So, the Jews are tolerated here, permitted to remain as long as they keep their Judaism private. It's an arrangement you find acceptable. You live well, but of course you can only practice the Jewish religion privately. No one bothers you. To be sure, the King can expel you anytime he wants, but you have learned to live with insecurity. Meanwhile, England is better than Spain!

END

98

The ship weighs anchor and sails across the English Channel. At Rotterdam, you decide to go ashore and continue on to Amsterdam. You find a small but flourishing Jewish community. That settles it! Holland is your final destination.

Since many guilds were closed to Jews your choice is limited, so you learn the trade of making eyeglasses and become very skilled. As you grow older and more established, you look to marry. You fall in love with a member of another Spanish Jewish family, *de Spinoza*. A marriage is arranged. Soon a son is born, and you feel so fortunate and blessed that you call him *Baruch de Spinoza*.

END

99

You select the ship of an English explorer. It takes you to the New World. When you arrive in the wilderness, friendly Indians meet you. You settle among them, observe your Jewish ways, and live quietly. Because there are no other Jews, you marry an Indian and have several children.

In the fall, you look at your family and crops. Life is good. Living in a quonset hut, you try to think of how to thank God properly. You remember the festival of *Sukot*. What a beautiful festival for a wanderer like you! You build a small booth and recite whatever prayers you can remember. All of your family eat in the *sukah* for a week. The Indians come to look. They ask you what this is all about.

You tell them the story of how the Israelites left Egypt and lived in booths for forty years. "Ever since that time," you say, "my people have thanked God for the harvest and for their freedom in the same way." As you look out over the shimmering waters of Narragansett Bay, you feel very good. "I may be far away from Jews, but I feel close; I have kept the faith of my people, even in this New World!"

END

100

The island settlement is isolated. Ships come from Europe once or twice a year, but mostly you are on your own.

The Spanish soldiers consider the natives to be savages. They turn them into slaves, steal their gold, and mistreat them constantly. The natives learn to hate white people with a quiet, but relentless, fury. The Spaniards are so greedy for gold that they never notice the hatred. When you try to warn them, they laugh at your fear.

One day, a large, armed party of natives surrounds the Spanish settlement. They lead you and the other Spaniards to their village. "White man here before," says the chief. Some of them are still there, you notice, from the number of skulls piled outside their temple.

It's too late. The natives circle around you, their ceremonial knives gleaming.

END

101

Finally, you and some other refugees join the settlers of a new colony in Peru. Life is hard, but acceptable. No one inquires about your personal life, and you can practice Judaism privately. Outwardly, you pretend to be a Catholic.

After many, many years, you feel totally secure. There is no separate *Inquisition* in Peru, but the Bishop of Lima has established a special court to inquire into the lives of *Conversos*. Because they believe that you are really a Jew, the *Inquisitors* look at you very carefully. Quickly, they discover your secret Judaism and arrest you. In chains, you are placed aboard the next ship and sent back to Spain. The end seems inevitable.

☞   *Go to page 77.*

102

The wedding reception should be at your home, but *Señor de Naxos* persuades you to let him provide it. Their home is a showplace. The courtyard of their palace is decked out in gorgeous lanterns and flowers. Servants move silently among the guests, helping everyone to the excellent food. The host smiles at everyone and welcomes people.

Suddenly, the sky darkens and rain begins to fall. There is confusion in the courtyard as the guests run for cover. Quick-witted servants help the bride and bridegroom into the great hall of the *de Naxos* palace. You put your arm around your spouse of many years. "May God bless and protect our child," you whisper fervently.

END

103

The party at your home is lovely. Everyone enjoys the food and the entertainment of jugglers and acrobats. You rise to make an announcement.

"Friends, tonight we have gathered for a truly blessed occasion. In honor of our newly-married couple, I shall present a new *Torah* to our synagogue, B'nai Sepharad. Whenever we worship, we shall be reminded that all of us fled Spain in order to be faithful to the *Torah*. We wish for our children a twofold blessing: faith in our *Torah* and faith in one another."

END

104

Careful preparations must be made for the trip to France. You choose bolts of the finest brocades, laces, and velvet. You pack buttons and buckles of ivory, silver, and gold; you even include special needles and threads. Heaven only knows what might be available in a country so depressed that its king must send all the way to Turkey for a tailor.

Your last act is to bid goodbye to the *Sultan*. You ask his permission to leave, explaining to him that it would be a good deed to bring civilized clothing to the French. He wishes you luck.

The only ship available is an English man-of-war. The captain is glad to have a passenger; he looks forward to good conversation and pleasant company. However, he explains that he will be sailing through the Mediterranean without stopping and directly to England. He tells you that he is ordered to dock at one of the *Cinque Ports*, Rye, and that you'll have no trouble finding transportation to France. "Why," he exclaims, "there are boats going back and forth to Calais every day!"

☞ *Turn to page 108.*

105

One day, you receive word that the *Sultan* of Turkey will visit Jerusalem. He has requested a guide, and you have been appointed. What an opportunity!

When he arrives, you are brought into his presence. After you bow, he asks you to teach him and his children about the city. You must be very careful not to offend him. He is a Moslem, and you are a Jew. Sometimes the same fact means different things to different people. You want to be sure to explain everything so that you are truthful, but without challenging what he believes.

The highlight of his pilgrimage is his visit to the *Dome of the Rock*, a mosque built over the spot where, according to legend, *Mohammed* ascended into heaven.

He is so pleased with your teaching that he commands you to go to Constantinople with him. Since he controls Palestine as well as his own country, you cannot refuse. You spend the rest of your life there, serving as tutor to the royal children.

END

106

Every year, you make a tour of the Jewish communities around the Mediterranean Sea. With your assistants, you visit Fustat (Cairo) and Alexandria in Egypt, Tunis and Algiers in North Africa, Marseilles in France, Venice and Soncino in Italy, Athens and Salonika in Greece, and Constantinople in Turkey. The voyage takes you eight months. In each place, you teach about the *Holy Land* and collect money to support Jewish life there.

When you die, your grave is placed just outside the Golden Gate of Jerusalem's ancient walls. According to Jewish legend, this is the best possible place to be buried. When the *Messiah* finally comes and revives the dead, you will be at the head of the line to enter the holy city.

END

107

As you sit reading the ancient books of your people
you remember the legend that studying the *Kabbalah*
can be dangerous. Even the *Talmud* records that several
ancient scholars who probed too deeply into the realm of
mystical knowledge either went mad or like the prophet
Elijah were swept away by angels. You do not believe in
such superstitions and continue your studies, enjoying
the respect your family and friends pay you as a man
of learning.

E N D

108

When you arrive in Calais, you go to the nearest tavern. They tell you that a stagecoach leaves for Paris every day. The trip will take nearly two days.

Paris is a beautiful city with wide avenues and many parks. The gardens are filled with colorful flowers and bushes in the shapes of animals. You take your time, walking past tall buildings which have graceful columns and stonework. Finally you arrive at the Royal Palace.

You present your letter of invitation, and a uniformed page leads you to your room. "His Majesty will send for you when he is ready," he says. You pace back and forth in your room. Finally, you are summoned. This page is even more splendidly dressed than the first, and you begin to realize that it was wrong to imagine that French people do not know what beautiful clothes are.

When you are ushered into the throne room, you bow very low. As you look up, your eyes blink. The glitter of gold and jewels flashes brightly. The King commands: "Tailor, we have brought you here to create costumes for our Turkish masked ball. The entire court shall be dressed as in your land. If you please us, we shall reward you handsomely and send you home. Now, go!"

You work harder than you've ever worked before, and the King's party is a success. He gives you a purse of gold coins and a large, precious jewel. Soldiers escort you to Marseilles, where a ship is waiting for you. When you arrive back in Constantinople, you are really glad to be home, but the adventure was fun.

END

109

You decide that kabbalistic studies are too dangerous. Something very unusual seems to be happening, and you want to leave before the consequences are unpleasant. Your fellow students tell you that you're imagining things. "Nothing's going to happen to you. Studying the *Zohar* is the same as studying any other book," they say.

You don't agree. The risks are too great. You pack your belongings onto a cart drawn by a donkey and head southward to Jerusalem, where you enter an academy with a more typical course of study.

☞   *Turn to page 63.*

110

You run into the street and call the police over to your shop. "Thank God you are here," you say. "A fearful pirate left this silver with me. He wants me to buy it, and he will be back in a few hours. But it would not be right for me to deal in stolen property. Take the silver back to the Duke!"

The police carry the silver away, but leave three men hiding in your shop. When the pirate returns, he pulls out his sword. Three against one is too much, however. Soon, he lies on the sidewalk—one less pirate to steal from honest people.

The Duke sends for you. "What reward do you want?" he asks. "I need no reward, Your Grace. Our *Torah* says: 'Lo tignov,' 'You shall not steal.' I would not have been faithful to God or to Judaism if I had kept the silver." He is impressed with your answer, but he insists on giving you a golden ring. "I know that Jewish people are sometimes treated badly. If someone bothers you, just hold up this ring. It means that you will always be under my protection. No one will ever harm you."

You bow and back out of his presence. Now you know that you can live happily and safely in Nantes for as long as you want.

END

GLOSSARY

Aboab Family • Famous and distinguished Spanish Jewish family, many of whom moved to Holland in 1942. Descendants of this family also became leaders of the New World Jewish community, including Isaac Aboab, one of the first rabbis to come to the colonies.

Abravanel, Isaac (1437–1509) • Senior advisor to Spain's King Ferdinand. He tried to prevent the expulsion by a payment of money. Isabella refused. Later served as financial advisor to Italian cities. Wrote books on Bible and philosophy.

Ajunto • Ladino word for a group of people (board) governing a congregation in the Sephardic or Mediterranean Jewish world.

Alkabetz, Solomon (c. 1505–1584) • Mystic and colleague of Joseph Karo, who lived in Safed during the sixteenth century. Wrote "Lechah Dodi" and many other poems, songs, and books.

Allah • Name of God in Islamic religion.

Amidah • Central prayers of the Jewish worship service.

Ashkenazi, Solomon (1520–1600) • Jewish physician and diplomat. Born in Italy and settled in Turkey in 1564. Performed diplomatic services for the Grand Vizier, including negotiating peace between Venice and Turkey and securing the revocation of the decree expelling Jews from Venice in 1571.

Auto-da-fé • "Act of Faith." During this public ceremony, people who had been found guilty by the Inquisition were forced to confess their sins and were punished, either by whipping, embarrassment, fines, imprisonment, expulsion, or, for the worst cases, burning at the stake.

Barbary Coast • Northern coast of Africa from Morocco to Tunisia controlled by the Barbary Pirates from the sixteenth century to the middle of the nineteenth century.

Barbary Pirates • Best known as one cause of the American Mediterranean expedition during the War of 1812, these unsavory ruffians had been around for years, raiding ships and running back to their hiding places on the coast of North Africa.

Basques • Inhabitants of the Pyrénées.

Bible • The sacred book of the Jewish people containing the legends, laws, and history of Judaism in twenty-four books arranged in three sections: the Torah or Five Books of Moses, the Prophets, and the Writings. In the Christian version these sections are referred to as the Old Testament.

Caesarea • Port city of Israel, which dates back before the Common Era, occupied at various times by the Seleucids, the Egyptians, and the Romans.

Cardinal de Sourdes • A real person. The locations have been changed to fit the story-line, but the events are true. They happened to the author's family, which still owns the snuffbox.

Castile • The central part of Spain, united with Aragon after 1479 to make a single kingdom through the marriage of Ferdinand and Isabella.

Chazan • Hebrew term for cantor.

Chevrah Gemilut Chasadim • A Jewish society which provided for poor people by distributing food, money, clothing, and other necessary items.

Cinque Ports • Five seacoast towns on the southeastern shore of England facing France.

Converso • Term used for those Jews who converted to Catholicism in order to remain in Spain.

Crusader • A soldier in the service of Christian armies sent from Europe to win control of Palestine from the Moslems during the Middle Ages. The Crusaders were notorious for their unprovoked attacks upon Jewish civilians in Europe and the Middle East.

David • Second king of Israel who united the kingdoms of Judah and Israel and moved his capital to Jerusalem, thereafter called the "City of David." As a boy he killed the Philistine warrior Goliath and in later life is credited with writing most of the biblical Book of Psalms.

De Naxos, Joseph Nasi (c. 1520–1579) • Head of an international trading family with branches in Holland, Italy, and Turkey. Political advisor to sultans, he was named Duke of Naxos in 1566 and gained great power. Despite intrigues against him, he retained his power and protected Turkish Jewry. He tried unsuccessfully to rebuild the city of Tiberias as a refuge for Jews and as a manufacturing city in Palestine.

De Spinoza • The Spinoza family were Portuguese Marranos who settled in Holland. Their son Baruch (1632–1677) was a philosopher whose unorthodox opinions resulted in his excommunication from the Jewish community in 1656. He was also an optometrist. Baruch means "blessed."

Destruction of the Temple • See "Ninth of Av."

Dome of the Rock • In Jerusalem, now site of a special mosque on the Temple Mount. Mohammed, Islam's chief prophet, supposedly ascended to heaven from this spot.

Dominican Monks • During the twelfth century, Dominicans in southern France burned Jewish books. Their feelings did not abate with the passage of time.

Elijah • Ancient Hebrew prophet who risked his life to banish pagan worship from the Kingdom of Israel during the ninth century B.C.E. According to the Bible, he did not die but was carried to heaven in a fiery chariot. In Jewish legend, Elijah will announce the coming of the Messianic Age.

Eretz Yisrael • "The Land of Israel."

Erev Shabbat • Friday afternoon, just before the Jewish Sabbath begins; a time of special preparation for the Sabbath.

Ferdinand and Isabella • After 1479, the kingdoms of Aragon and Castile were unified. The Moslems or Moors were pushed into North Africa. The unification permitted Spain to begin colonial exploration and to agree to the Inquisition's long-held belief that only Catholics should live in Spain. Jews, who were helpful in the period before unification, were no longer necessary and could, therefore, be expelled. Confiscation of their property also brought a financial bonus to the Church and the Crown.

Grand Inquisitor • See "Inquisition."

Havdalah • The service which ends the Sabbath on Saturday night and separates the Sabbath from the following week.

Henry VII • King of England from 1485 to 1509. Although Jews were not legally supposed to live in England between 1290 and 1656, the kings of England permitted them to enter because they were famous as good businessmen.

Holy Land • Israel.

Inquisition • Given its major impetus under Pope Innocent III in 1198, the Inquisition continued until it was finally dissolved permanently in 1834. A specifically national Inquisition for Spain, without papal help, was founded by Ferdinand and Isabella in 1480. The basic function of the Inquisition was to assure proper belief and practice among people who were already Catholic. They were especially interested in Jews who converted and who might be involved in heresy. Only later, after the expulsion, did they become concerned with Jews who might lead Catholics to sin. The Inquisitor executes the Inquisition's orders. The name of its most notorious Chief or Grand Inquisitor, Torquemada, is almost synonymous with torture, oppression, and ruthlessness.

Inquisitor • See "Inquisition."

Judaizer • A Converso who pretended to practice Catholicism but who secretly kept some of the Jewish ways. Many people were brought before the Inquisition's court, accused of being Judaizers, and convicted. It is not certain, but it is probable, that many of these accusations were false, made up so that the person's money could be taken or so that he or she could be thrown out of a good job.

Kabbalah • The major form of Jewish mysticism (secret knowledge of the universe and God). According to the Talmud, when four second-century scholars probed too deeply into the Kabbalah, one looked into heaven and died, one lost his mind, and a third entered Paradise but cut down all the plants. Only the fourth returned from his mystical journey. While very old, it became more popular after the expulsion from Spain, when Jews tried to explain what had happened to them. The center of sixteenth-century Kabbalistic study was northern Palestine.

Kai-feng-fu • See "Sinkiang."

Karo, Joseph (1488–1575) • Leader of Palestinian kabbalists in the sixteenth century. He wrote the *Shulchan Aruch*, a law book which still governs traditional Jewish life.

Marrano • A term meaning "pig" which was used to mock Jews who had converted to Catholicism in Spain.

Messiah • God's Anointed One who, according to various Jewish traditions, will establish a Golden Age on earth.

Midrash • A vast body of literature, generally non-legal, dealing with philosophy, theology, ethics, folkways, and anecdotes. Most collections are dated from the third to the tenth centuries C.E.

Mitzvah • Literally, a divine commandment. Generally means an act of philanthropy or human compassion toward others; a good deed.

Mohammed • Chief prophet and founder of Islam.

Nieto, David (1654–1728) • Early leader of British Jewry, descendant of a Spanish family who originally moved to Italy. Wrote several important scholarly works.

Ninth of Av (Tishah b'Av) • Ninth day of the Hebrew month of Av which occurs in July or August. A Jewish fast day recalling the destruction of the First Temple in 586 B.C.E. by the Babylonians and of the Second Temple in 70 C.E. by the Romans. The date was chosen deliberately for the expulsion from Spain in order to add more insult and humiliation. C.E. (Common Era) is a term used by Jews instead of Anno Domine (A.D.) which orders the calendar according to the life of Jesus. B.C.E. stands for Before the Common Era.

Parnas • The non-rabbinic leader or president of a synagogue.

Pesach • The festival of Passover, usually in April, in which Jews recall the Exodus from Egypt and pledge to help people everywhere become free.

Roland • The French military hero immortalized in the medieval epic poem, *La Chanson de Roland* (The Song of Roland). As commander of Charlemagne's forces, he was killed in the Pyrénées by Basques as Charlemagne's army returned to France after its invasion of Spain in 778.

Shabbat • The Sabbath; Friday sunset to Saturday sunset.

Shacharit • The early morning prayer service in the synagogue.

Shalom • A greeting word which means "peace."

Shema • Hebrew for "Hear," the title and first word of Judaism's most important prayer, "Hear, O Israel, the Lord is our God, the Lord is One."

Sinkiang • A western province of China. Kai-feng-fu is a city in Sinkiang where Jews, probably from a caravan like Marco Polo's, settled. They continued to live there until about 1900. Their documents are preserved at the Hebrew Union College-Jewish Institute of Religion, Cincinnati, Ohio.

Snuffbox • A small, usually ornate box used to carry snuff, a powdered tobacco that is either chewed or inhaled.

Solomon • Son and successor of King David. He built the First Temple in Jerusalem, was renowned for his wisdom, and is credited with writing the Song of Songs, Ecclesiastes, and Psalm 72 of the Bible.

Star of David • The six-pointed star which serves as a symbol of loyalty for Jews.

Sukah • A booth decorated with branches, fruits, and vegetables that celebrants dine in during the festival of Sukot.

Sukot • Festival of Booths or Tabernacles which usually occurs late in September or early in October. Recalls both God's goodness through the harvest and the Exodus from Egypt.

Sultan • Turkey's equivalent of a king.

Talit Katan • A small prayer shawl worn by traditional Jews under their shirts to remind themselves of God and His commandments.

Talmud • A collection of Jewish law and practice. There are two compilations, the Babylonian Talmud and the Palestinian Talmud. The most important, the Babylonian Talmud, was written in Babylonia about 500 C.E. and serves until the present as the basis of traditional Judaism.

Torah • God's law or teaching; the first five books of the Bible in a special scroll.

Tsedakah • Righteousness or charity.

Zion • A hill and fortress in the center of Jerusalem that has come to stand for all of Israel.

Zohar • The central kabbalistic book believed by some to have been written by Moses de Leon in Spain in 1245 C.E., believed by others to have been written as early as the second century.